3 1160 00269 5950

SO-CFJ-687

The Take-Along Dog

by BARBARA ANN PORTE

pictures by
EMILY ARNOLD McCULLY

 Greenwillow Books, New York

Watercolor paints and a black pen
were used for the full-color art.
The text type is Clearface.

Printed in Singapore by Tien Wah Press
First Edition   10 9 8 7 6 5 4 3 2 1

Library of Congress Cataloging-in-Publication Data
Porte, Barbara Ann.
The take-along dog/by Barbara Ann Porte;
pictures by Emily Arnold McCully.
p.   cm.
Summary: Because Mother does not like dogs,
Sam and Abigail must take Benton with them
everywhere, including trying to sneak him into
the movies, the library, and the swimming pool.
ISBN 0-688-08053-7.   ISBN 0-688-08054-5 (lib. bdg.)
[1. Dogs—Fiction.]   I. McCully, Emily Arnold, ill.
II. Title.   PZ7.P7995Tak 1989
[E]—dc19   88-18775   CIP   AC

For Carolyn and Ken,

Deborah and Brian,

with love

Sam and I are going to the swimming pool. "Hurry up, Abigail," my brother tells me. He's worried he'll be late for his swimming lesson. When I was Sam's age, I worried too. "I'm coming," I say. Benton, our dog, is coming with us. I pick him up and put him in my beach bag.

Sam and I take Benton everywhere. We have to.
Our mother is afraid of dogs. When Daddy
brought him home last week, he said,
"I used to have a dog. Her name
was Lou. 'Yoo-hoo, Lou,' my
mother used to call her."

Our mother said, "Really? There used to be a dog next door when I was growing up. It was a big spotted dog that was always barking. 'Stay away,' my mother said. 'A dog that barks like that is probably up to no good.' I listened to my mother."

6

"Probably," said Daddy, "your mother meant a <u>big</u> dog. Benton is such a little dog you'll forget he's even here."

"We'll see," said Mother. "In the meantime, when the three of you are gone, don't leave your dog with me."

Daddy, Sam, and I agreed. When all of us go out, one of us takes Benton. I don't know what will happen in the fall, when Sam and I go back to school.

"Don't worry," Daddy says. "By then Mom and Benton will be friends." I hope he's right.

Right now, Daddy is at work. That is why Benton is going with us to the swimming pool.

I spread my towel on the grass, lie down, and
put my beach bag next to me. Sam jumps into
the pool for his swimming lesson. He is up to
the dead man's float.

Just as Sam begins to blow bubbles, Benton climbs
out of my beach bag, runs to the pool, and jumps
in. I am surprised at how well he can swim.
The lifeguard blows his whistle. "Whose dog is
that?" he yells.

"Mine," says Sam. "His name is Benton."

"I don't care what his name is." The lifeguard is
shouting. "I want him out of the pool this minute.
Dogs are not even allowed inside the fence. Take
him home NOW!!!"

"He didn't have to shout," Sam says as we leave.
"He could have said 'please.'"

Sam and I go to the library in the afternoon for
Summer Reading Club. Benton goes, too, in my
book bag.
"Shhh," I tell him, "please. There's no barking in
the library."

Ms. Alberico, the librarian, is already listening to reports. We sit at a table.

Just as Sam begins to tell about a story we read,
about a spider named Anansi, Benton climbs out
of my book bag, onto the table.

"Abigail," Ms. Alberico says, "I myself like dogs, but
   they're not allowed in the library."
"Yes, Ms. Alberico," I say. "But Benton didn't bark."
"No dogs at all is the rule," says Ms. Alberico. "The
   rule does not say anything about 'no barking dogs.'

"Come back next week," she says as we leave.
"Just you, Abigail, and your brother."

We stop for ice cream on the way home. "No food!
No pets! No bare feet!" reads the sign in the
window. I wait outside with Benton. Sam goes in
with the money. He buys two vanilla cones with
sprinkles. He eats one. Benton and I eat the other.

The next day it rains. We go to the movies. My
raincoat has extra-large pockets. I tuck Benton
into one of them.

"Fearless Frieda and the Five-Fanged Outlaw," reads
the sign above the movie house. It does not say a
word about dogs.

"Two, please," I tell the woman in the ticket booth.
I pay for the tickets and we go inside. I buy two
bags of buttered popcorn, extra-large. I give one
to Sam. "If you don't bark," I tell Benton, "you
can have some of mine."

Benton doesn't bark. He is too busy watching the
picture on the screen and eating popcorn to make
noise.

Then, halfway through the movie, just as
Fearless Frieda is about to capture the Five-Fanged
Outlaw and all of the popcorn is gone, Benton
climbs out of my pocket, stands up on my lap, and
starts barking.

"Shhh," say some of the children.
"Isn't he cute?" say some of the others.
All of them together are making quite
a commotion.

"Excuse me," says a woman in a uniform.
"Dogs are not allowed at the movies. You'll
 have to leave."
"But we already paid," I explain.
"I'm sorry," she says, "but a rule is a rule."
"Yes," I say, "but there's no sign." I mean no
 sign about dogs, but she misunderstands.
 She points to a sign as we leave. "No refunds,"
 it reads.

"Do you want to know how the movie ends?" I ask Sam on our way home. Sam does. I make up an ending and tell him.

"Fearless Frieda draws fangs on her face," I tell him, "and puts on an outlaw costume. The real outlaw falls in love with her. After that, it is easy for Fearless Frieda to capture him and put him in a cage. That's it," I say.

"That's all?" asks Sam.

I think about it.

"Wait," I say, "there's more. Fearless Frieda is surprised to discover that the Five-Fanged Outlaw is really a child. 'Where are your parents?' she asks. He tells her that he is an orphan. Fearless Frieda takes him home with her. She dresses him in regular clothes, files down his fangs, and sends him to school. After some time passes, the Five-Fanged Outlaw reforms. When he grows up he becomes a teacher. Sometimes he tells the children stories about his outlaw days, and how he was captured by Fearless Frieda."

"That's better," says Sam.

"Did you have a good time at the movies?"
our mother asks when we get home.
"Fine, thank you," I say. "Except Benton got
bored so we had to leave early."

The next day is Sunday. We all go to the park for a picnic—our mother and father, Sam, Benton, and I. We take tuna fish sandwiches and chocolate cake. Also, lemonade in a thermos. We take dog food for Benton.

After we play Frisbee and eat, Sam and I go for a
ride on the merry-go-round. Our father comes
with us to watch. Benton is asleep.

"Hold down the fort," our father tells our mother.
"We'll be back before Benton wakes up."

Sam rides a horse. I ride an elephant.

"Can we ride again?" Sam asks when the

merry-go-round stops.

"One more time," says Daddy. Sam climbs

off the horse and onto the giraffe.

"I'll go check on Benton," I say.

Just as I come in sight of our picnic blanket, I hear
a loud commotion. Then I see a large spotted dog.
It is barking and racing straight toward Mother.
I start to run, but I am too far away to help.

Just then, Benton wakes up. He starts barking
and jumping up and down on the picnic blanket.
The big dog stops. It stops in its tracks. It stops
so fast, it almost falls on its face. It tucks its tail
between its legs, turns around, and runs away.

"Good dog, Benton," I hear my mother say as I
reach them. "You are a good, brave dog." She pats
him. Benton looks surprised. He licks her hand.
I sit on the blanket and wait for my mother to
catch her breath.

Daddy and Sam come back.

"Benton and I had a very close call," Mother tells
them. Then she tells us all about the other dog.
"It was the spitting image," she says, "of the dog
that lived next door when I was Sam's age. If

Benton had not been so brave, I don't know
what might have happened."

"That big dog sounds a lot like my dog, Lou," says
Daddy. "My mother used to say, 'You're a good
dog, Lou, but I'll eat my hat if you're not afraid of
your own shadow.'"

The next day is Monday. Sam has a ballet lesson in the afternoon. I walk with him to class. Our mother says, as we are leaving, "Why don't you leave Benton home with me?"

"Alone?" I ask. "Just the two of you?"

"Why not?" she says. "I could use a good, small, brave dog like Benton to keep me company."

"I guess Daddy was right," I tell Sam. I mean about Mom and Benton becoming friends. Sam looks disappointed.

"I guess that means," he says, "we won't get to take Benton to school."

"You know what?" Sam says

  as we walk home from ballet class.

"What?" I answer.

"I can take Benton to school for Show and Tell.

  I'll take him in my book bag. 'This dog is very

  brave,' I'll tell my class. 'This dog is not afraid of

      a shouting lifeguard,

      a five-fanged outlaw,

      or a large spotted dog that is barking.

"'Benton is the bravest small dog in the world.'
That's what I'll tell them."